A DANCER'S DREAM

For Rose - **K.W.**

For my sister, Jess - **L.S.**

The text in this book is an abridged version of the story,
'Casse-Noisette' by Katherine Woodfine,
originally published in the anthology *Winter Magic*.

SIMON & SCHUSTER

First published in Great Britain in 2020
by Simon & Schuster UK Ltd
1st Floor, 222 Gray's Inn Road, London WC1X 8HB
This paperback edition published in 2022

A CIP catalogue record for this book is available from the British Library upon request

ISBN: 978-1-4711-8615-8 (HB)
ISBN: 978-1-4711-8616-5 (EB)
ISBN: 978-1-4711-8614-1 (PB)
Printed in China
1 3 5 7 9 10 8 6 4 2

MIX
Paper from
responsible sources
FSC® C008047
FSC
www.fsc.org

THE REAL STORY OF
THE NUTCRACKER

A DANCER'S DREAM

KATHERINE WOODFINE
& LIZZY STEWART

SIMON & SCHUSTER
London   New York   Sydney   Toronto   New Delhi

Stana gazed out of the window at the softly falling snow. It was only two weeks until Christmas, and it had been snowing all day long: now the blue-and-green tiled roofs and gold domes of St. Petersburg looked as though they had been spread with a thick white blanket.

"Come away from the window, Stana," scolded Mademoiselle. Stana turned away from the window. After two years at the Imperial Ballet School, she knew better than to disobey the governess. But how could she rest? She had been in a fever of excitement since she had first heard that they were auditioning for the role of Clara, the young girl in the Mariinsky Theatre's new ballet. It was certainly a rare and special role. Students at the ballet school did sometimes play tiny parts in the ballets, but for a pupil to play a leading role was unheard of.

"They're looking for a girl of twelve years old to play the part of Clara — that's the same age as us!" her best friend Anna had whispered to her in the dormitory. Somehow, Anna always managed to find out everything first.

The ballet was to be called *The Nutcracker*, although Stana liked the title better in French. In Russian, *The Nutcracker* sounded spiky and hard; in French, the words *Le Casse-Noisette* were as soft as snowflakes, sweet as a Christmas sugar plum melting on her tongue.

The words tinkled, like the notes of Mr Tchaikovsky's music. When Stana had first heard that music, she had known that she wanted to play Clara. The glistening notes of the piano had swept her far away from the Imperial Ballet School; away from lessons and walks around the garden two by two; away from lying awake in the dormitory at night, whispering with Anna about her poorly sister, Olga, or worrying about how Mama would be able to pay the doctor's bills.

When she heard the music she was stepping through a pine forest, glittering with frost in the moonlight, her footsteps crunching in the snow. She was gliding through St. Petersburg's most elegant ballroom.

Then she felt the warmth of the fire against her face, she saw the candles on the Christmas tree, Mama's homemade gingerbread angels and she was kneeling on the rug with Olga, drinking tea with jam.

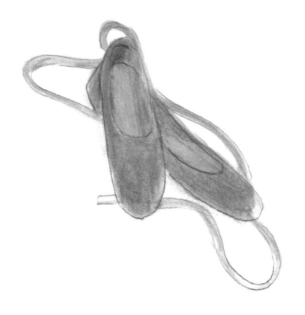

One day, word had flown around the school: Petipa, the ballet master, was coming to watch them dance, and to choose who would play Clara. But Stana was distracted. A letter had come from Mama that morning: they had taken Olga to the hospital. "Whatever is the matter with you?" hissed Anna, but there was no time to answer. Petipa had arrived.

It was strange to see the first ballet master here in the ordinary surroundings of the practice room. As the girls each swept their most reverent curtsey, Petipa strutted before them, looking them carefully up and down in turn. He was an old man now, but his eyes were sharp, and he was still as dapper as ever in his smartly cut suit. Following a little way behind him was the second ballet master, Mr Ivanov, and to her surprise, Stana saw that sitting at the piano, was the composer, Mr Tchaikovsky. She knew all about him, of course: he was one of the most famous composers in all Russia. But here in the school practice room, he looked surprisingly ordinary – just another old man with white hair and a tired face. People said he had not been the same since his sister died.

"Now, mademoiselles, shall we begin?" announced Petipa. Excited and eager to prove themselves, the girls began to dance. "You must *feel* the music," he told them, looking from one to the other keenly.

"Do you not see the pictures that Mr Tchaikovsky has painted for you?" Suddenly, he pointed to Stana. "You — little girl. Tell me what you see when you dance to this music."

Stana flushed scarlet. She felt tongue-tied, but she knew that this was her big chance. She thought of Tchaikovsky's music again, and she was able to give Petipa an answer — a snowy pine forest, a grand, gilded ballroom, the warm fire and the Christmas tree, her sister safe at home.

After she had finished, there was a moment of echoing silence, then Petipa nodded. "Très bon, mademoiselle. You must all use your imaginations like this when you dance, *oui*?"

He waved a hand to Tchaikovsky at the piano, and they all began to dance again, Stana feeling at once lighter and more purposeful than she had before.

She knew that she must have danced well, because Anna would hardly speak to her after they had finished, and flounced out of the room without waiting for her. Anna always wanted to be the best at everything, and she could not bear anyone else being the centre of attention – not even her best friend.

Anna often reminded Stana of Olga.

Olga might be three years younger than Stana, but she had always been intent on keeping pace with her big sister. She wanted to do whatever Stana did. And just like Anna, she was fierce as a tiger, flaring out into a fiery temper when she could not keep up. She had long been impatient to come to study at the Imperial Ballet School, like Stana. That had been before she was ill, of course. Stana knew that there would be no ballet for Olga now.

That thought had only just crossed Stana's mind when she realised, rather to her astonishment, that Mr Tchaikovsky himself was standing before her. For a moment she felt alarmed by his sudden appearance. But when he spoke, his voice was unexpectedly gentle:

"You answered Petipa's question well," he said. "Tell me, are you fond of music?"

She stared up at him, too surprised to know quite how to answer. "Very," she said at last.

"You said the music made you think of Christmas and that you imagined your little sister safe at home," he went on. "Where is your sister now?"

"She is in the hospital. She is very ill," Stana managed to reply.

He contemplated her for a moment. His eyes were large and sad, his expression quizzical, rather like an owl's. "I am sorry to hear that," he said, then he bowed and left the room.

o-one said any more to her about *The Nutcracker* that day, but a week later, Stana was told that she had been given the part of Clara. The other girls made a tremendous fuss about how envious they were. Anna stood a little to one side, her arms folded, saying nothing at all. Everyone was speculating about her costume and hair — but Stana did not care so very much.

It was the music that filled her with delight —
the music and the wonderful story of Clara,
who is given a nutcracker doll by her godfather,
Drosselmeyer, on Christmas Eve. After night
falls, the doll comes to life, and whisks her
away on a magical adventure. When Stana
played Clara, dancing to Tchaikovsky's music,
she became someone else — the heroine of a
marvellous fairy tale. Her worries all faded away.

She found herself inhabiting a world of
dancing sweets and flower-fairies. Spending
day after day at the theatre, she looked on,
entranced, as the spectacle came to life. As
Stana watched the stage being prepared, it was
not in the least difficult for her to conjure up
Clara's sense of enchantment and delight.

But rehearsals for *The Nutcracker* were not always easy. The days in the theatre were long and tiring. Petipa was ill, and after the first few rehearsals, Ivanov had to take his place. Stana felt very small among the company of grown-up dancers, and often, she wished that Anna was there with her. Before, they had always done everything together.

It was Mr Tchaikovsky, at the piano, who was a reassuring constant. Day after day, wonderful music flowed from his fingers. He was far too busy to speak to Stana, but she liked to know he was there. Once or twice he paused backstage to ask: "And how is your little sister? Is she getting well?"

Stana would curtsey and say: "She is still in the hospital, sir." She found it difficult to say any more. She hated even thinking of Olga, so small in the little hospital bed. Her skin looked pale and waxy, like a doll's. Her sister was sicker than ever and the hospital bills were terribly expensive.

There was nothing for Stana to do except dance. She practised harder than ever, grimly determined that she would be a success. She whispered promises in her head.

If I dance the first scene quite perfectly in the morning rehearsal, then Olga will be a little better. If Ivanov praises my dance with the nutcracker doll tomorrow, that means that Olga will begin to get well.

Before long, Olga and *The Nutcracker* had become tangled — twisted together like the satin ribbons on Stana's ballet shoes. Dancing as Clara was no longer an escape: it was a bargain, a promise, a trial like those that princes must perform in fairy stories. Stana worked hard, and then harder still. She was convinced that if she could only dance well, then Olga would be certain to get well, too — and they would all be able to have a happy Christmas.

Now, waiting for the curtain to rise on the first performance, Stana felt drawn tight, quivering like a violin string. Backstage at the Mariinsky, it smelled of excitement. Around her, the other pupils were laughing and chattering, thrilled to be staying up so long after their usual bedtime, and to have the chance to dance on the great stage. Stana envied them. She wished she could be excited: instead, she felt only frightened and as cold as the snow that was falling outside.

More than ever, she wished that Anna was here. Without her, Stana felt as though the edges of herself were being rubbed away. But most of all, Stana knew that Anna understood her. She already dreaded losing Olga – it felt as though she was losing Anna, too.

Almost, she wished that she had never been chosen for the role of Clara, and that she and Anna were both getting ready to perform ordinary roles in the ballet. Almost, she wished she had never heard the enchanted words *Le Casse-Noisette*, nor heard Tchaikovsky's haunting melodies. Almost, she wished she was back home, sitting with Olga on the rug in front of the fire, toasting their cheeks and drinking tea with jam.

Almost, but not quite.

She could hear the stirrings of the overture: the shimmering of the strings, the bright piping of the flutes rising above them, and all at once, her feet longed to dance.

"It's time to go," said Mademoiselle.

Waiting in the wings, ready for her cue, Stana lost herself in the rise and fall of the music. Beyond the stage, she could see the haze of the footlights, and then little glimpses of the audience, elegant ladies in furs and jewels, smart gentlemen in uniforms, and above all, the Tsar himself. But as the music swelled, it seemed to lift her up, as though she was being carried on magic wings.

And then she ran out onto the stage, into the bright glare of the lights. It was time to dance.

It was not until after midnight that the ballet finally drew to a close. As she took her curtain calls, she heard the clamour of the audience's applause, but all she could think was, *Have I done it?* Had she danced all right? Had she missed a step? Had she done enough to make Olga well again?

Backstage, the grown-up dancers were clapping each other on the back and shaking Ivanov by the hand. Tchaikovsky hurried by clutching a sheaf of sheet music scribbled all over in his spiky black handwriting. Among the tumult, he alone paused to give her a quick nod and a smile. At least he thought she had done well, Stana realised, with relief.

ut once she was in the dormitory, Stana found she could not sleep. She lay awake, staring into the dark, hearing the soft, rustling breaths of the other girls sleeping around her. The notes of Tchaikovsky's music were still racing around in her head. She heard the clock strike two, before at last she fell into a restless sleep — and when she slept, she began to dream.

She found herself back in the Mariinsky Theatre in her Clara costume. But now the auditorium was dark and empty. Then the music began — and Stana danced. She twirled and leaped with a springy lightness she had never experienced before; she felt she could dance forever.

This time Anna was there too, wearing the
glittering costume of the Sugar Plum Fairy,
dancing more beautifully than Stana
had ever seen her.

Ivanov performed the role of the Nutcracker Prince; and Mr Tchaikovsky was Drosselmeyer, his owl-face looking down at her from up in the clock.

All at once the music seemed to shatter.
The clock was striking again. *Time is running out,*
she heard Drosselmeyer say, and somehow she
knew that he was talking about Olga. All at
once, she knew she had to find her little sister;
that she was here, somewhere, among the
dancers. But Stana could not find her. She was
not among the gingerbread soldiers, nor the
rowdy army of mice.

The Mouse King tried to bar her way, but just as in the ballet, she hurled her satin shoe at him and he turned tail and vanished. Still she could not find Olga: she was not in the Palace of Sweets, nor among the dancers of chocolate and coffee and tea. She was not among the bonbons or the sugar candies, the hummingbirds or flower-fairies.

At last, Stana thought she caught a glimpse of Olga, dancing with the snowflakes, wearing a white tutu and a crown. She ran towards her, but even as she did so, the snowflakes seemed to whirl and blur before her eyes. At last, she stretched out her arms towards her sister, but her hands closed on nothing but air — not a dancer at all, but snowflakes, just the merest shape of a girl made of snow.

S tana woke up shivering and calling her sister's name, her heart pounding and the bedclothes tossed all about her like a stormy sea.

"What's the matter with you?" whispered Anna grumpily from the next bed.

"I had a nightmare," Stana whispered, her heart beginning to slow as she realised she was back at school, in the darkness of the dormitory.

"There's no need to start getting so dramatic, just because you played the part of Clara," said Anna sniffily. But she sounded more like her

usual self as she rolled over and said:
"Sssh, Stana. Let me go back to sleep."

Stana slept dreamlessly after that, and was still sound asleep when the rising bell rang, jolting her suddenly awake. The first performance was over, and it was another day just like any other: the bell tolling solemnly at eight o'clock, washing under the cold tap, dressing in their practice dresses and blue fringed shawls, having their hair combed by the maids.

"Stana had a nightmare last night," Anna reported to Lydia, who was known to be something of an expert on dreams, being the possessor of a dog-eared dream-book. "What was it about? Did you see a man in black? Were you running down a staircase?" asked Lydia.

But already, the dream was fading.

"No . . . I don't remember anything like that. I just remember that it was snowing . . ." said Stana uncertainly.

"Well, bad dreams do sometimes mean a change in the weather," said Lydia with a shrug.

"Hurry along now, girls, don't chatter," scolded Mademoiselle.

In every way, the morning was ordinary. It was as if the ballet itself had been only a dream, melting away to nothing at the sound of the rising bell. But by lunchtime, the first reviews of *The Nutcracker* had been published, and all at once everyone was talking about them:

"The *St. Petersburg Gazette* said it was 'tedious'," reported Nina, her eyes round.

"They said that Ivanov just copied Petipa's other ballets," sniffed another girl.

"They said that Antoinetta wasn't a bit like any kind of a fairy," added Anna.

"But she got five curtain calls!" argued someone else.

Stana put down her fork. She felt sick and she could scarcely touch her lunch. The ballet had not been a success; and as the day drew on, the news grew worse and worse. Some critics said the ballet was confusing, others that it was all spectacle and no substance. Some said it was not even a proper ballet. Even Tchaikovsky's beautiful music was criticised.

Stana herself was not left out. "The dance of student Stanislava Belinskaya with the injured nutcracker is quite unsuccessful both in composition and in execution," Nina read aloud from the newspaper.

"That's not fair," said Anna indignantly. "You danced it well!" Whether it was her nightmare or the bad reviews, Stana was not quite sure: but somehow in all this, Anna had forgiven her.

The fairy tale was over now; the sugar plum tasted bitter, not sweet. Stana's magic chance to shine had melted away. She felt dazed: she had danced as well as she knew how, and yet somehow it still had not been enough.

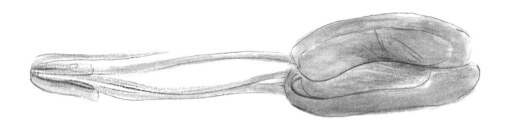

That afternoon, a letter arrived from Mama, and Stana ran up to the dormitory to open it. Anna followed behind her. Sitting on her bed, Stana tore open the envelope and shook out the note inside with trembling hands. It was only short — Mama wrote that she was sorry she had missed her performance, but there was good news. Olga had taken a turn for the better. There were still the bills to pay, of course, but the doctors said that with careful treatment, her sister would get well.

Stana stared at the words, a lump rising in her throat, and she seemed to hear the final triumphant chords and drumbeats of Tchaikovsky's music.

The Nutcracker had failed; but it did not matter. They would have a happy Christmas after all.

"What does it say?" asked Anna, dropping down beside her on the bed.

"She says that Olga is getting better," said Stana, trying to keep her voice from wobbling.

Anna pointed to something small, shining on Stana's pillow. "Look — what's that? Someone has left you a Christmas present!"

Stana put out a hand in surprise, and picked up a little note, folded and tied with a red and gold ribbon like a Christmas bonbon.

To her surprise, she saw that the label read, *For Clara*.

"What can it be?" asked Anna, leaning forward, eager and curious.

Stana unwrapped the crackling paper very slowly. Inside was a note, scribbled on a small slip of music manuscript paper. It was just four words, in the same spiky handwriting. *To help your sister*. Beside it was a hundred-rouble note. "A hundred roubles!" exclaimed Anna, her eyes wide. "But — who is it from? What does it mean?"

Stana's fingers traced the black, spidery writing. She thought she knew who it had come from — and exactly what it meant.

S tana could see the lights of Christmas trees in the houses across the street, she realised that she would soon be sitting with Mama and Olga, eating gingerbread angels and drinking tea with jam.

Fat, feathery snowflakes twirled and
pirouetted past the window, and there came
a faint jingling of bells outside — as light and
dainty as the dance of the Sugar Plum Fairy —
as the sleighs raced by, through the softly
falling snow.

AUTHOR'S NOTE

While this story is fictional, it is based on the real history of Tchaikovsky's famous ballet, *The Nutcracker*, which was first performed at the Mariinsky Theatre in St. Petersburg in December 1892. Just as in this story, the ballet was not at first a success, receiving mixed reviews from critics. Now, of course, it is one of the best-known and best-loved ballets of all time, and is performed all over the world each year at Christmas.

Twelve-year-old Stanislava Belinskaya, a student at the Imperial Ballet School, really was the first person to play the famous role of Clara in this very first production.

The real-life Stanislava actually did have a friend and classmate called Anna. If you know about the history of ballet, you may know that she grew up to be the world-famous ballerina — Anna Pavlova.

That first production of *The Nutcracker* had an open ending, leaving the audience wondering what would happen to Clara and the Nutcracker Prince. In later versions of the ballet, and in most productions you will see today, the ballet finishes with Clara waking up in her bedroom, and realising that her wonderful adventures with the nutcracker were only a dream after all.